WHO'S POORLY TOO?

The 'Get Well Soon' Book

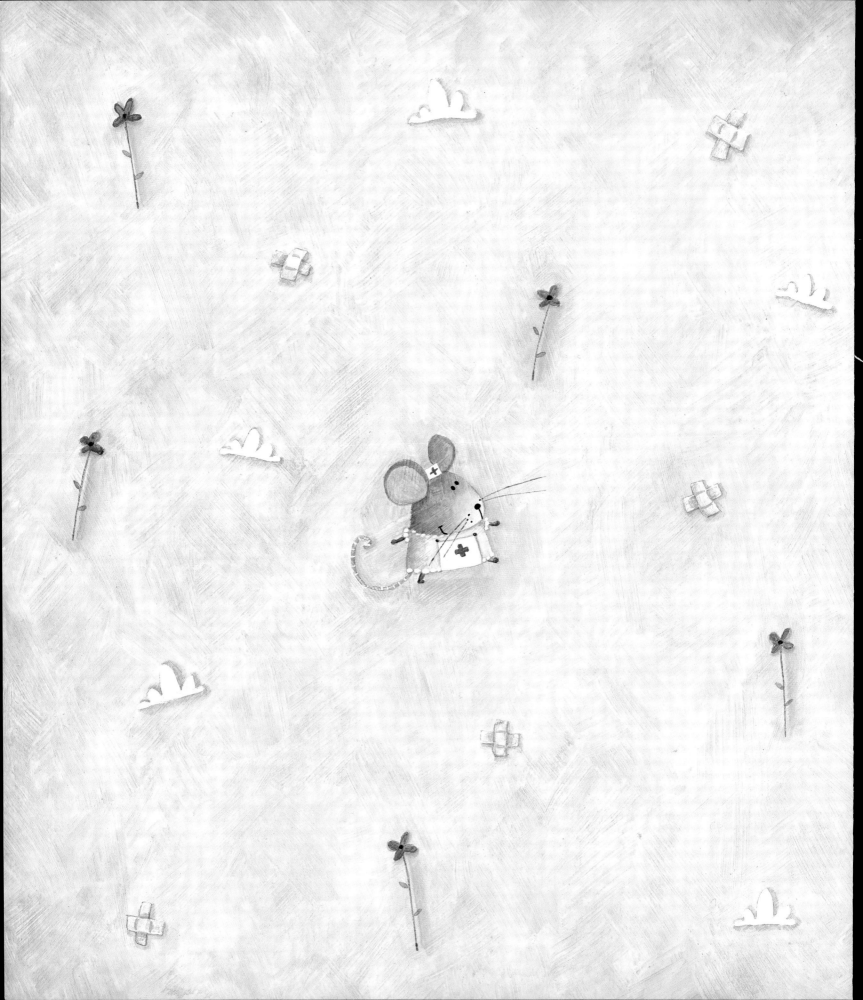

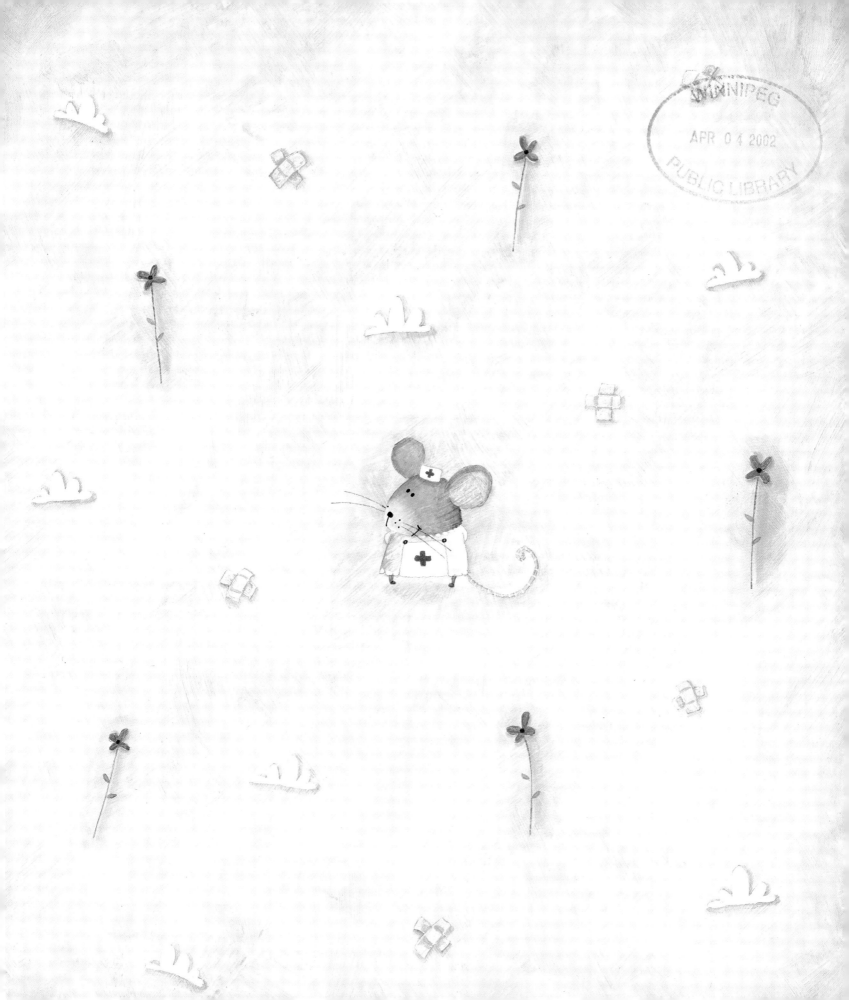

To all the poorly children in the world
K. G.

To my family
M. McQ.

A Red Fox Book

Published by Random House Children's Books
20 Vauxhall Bridge Road, London SW1V 2SA

A division of The Random House Group Ltd
London Melbourne Sydney Auckland
Johannesburg and agencies throughout the world

3 5 7 9 10 8 6 4 2

First published in Great Britain by The Bodley Head Children's Books 2000

Red Fox edition 2001

Printed and bound in Singapore

THE RANDOM HOUSE GROUP Limited Reg. No. 954009

www.randomhouse.co.uk

ISBN 0 09 940778 7

WHO'S POORLY TOO?

The 'Get Well Soon' Book

Kes Gray & Mary McQuillan

RED FOX

Cynthia the centipede is poorly.

She sprained 98 ankles playing hockey.

Hamish the hamster is poorly.

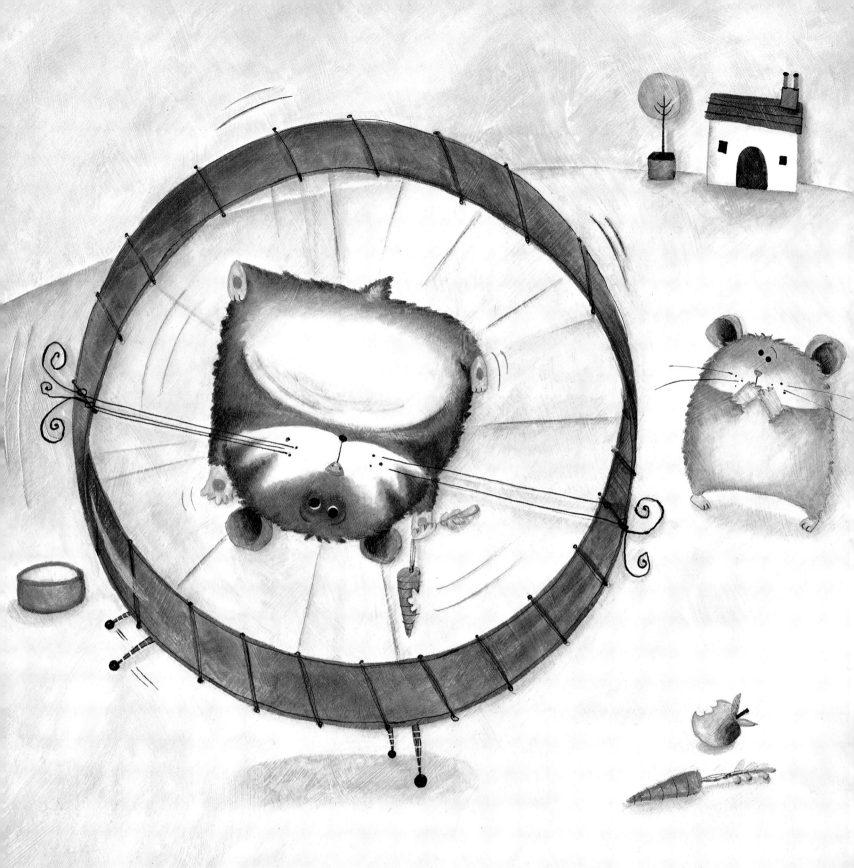

He got his whiskers caught up in his wheel.

Tiffany the tortoise is poorly.

An elephant trod on her shell.

Mohammed the mole is poorly.

He tunnelled straight into a well.

Dipak the dalmatian is poorly.

His spots came out in stripes.

Paul the python is poorly.

A gorilla tied him in a knot.

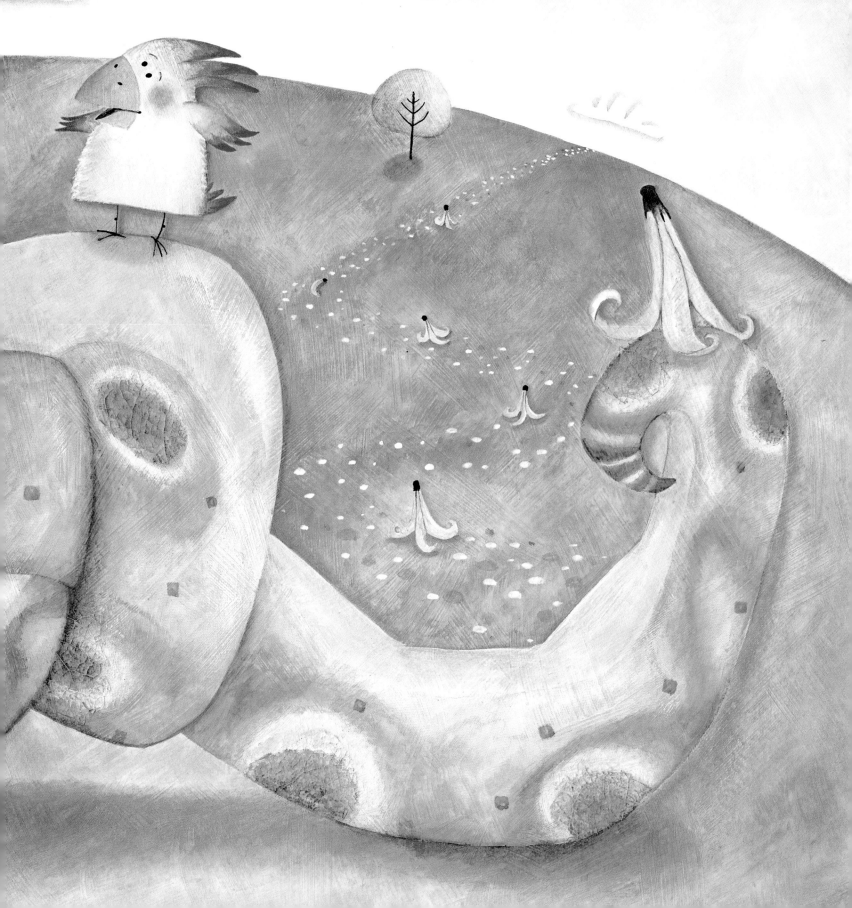

Cassie the cat is poorly.

She tried to chase a mouse through
a mouse hole.

Pedro the penguin is poorly.

He forgot to break the ice before diving in.

Connie the crocodile is poorly.

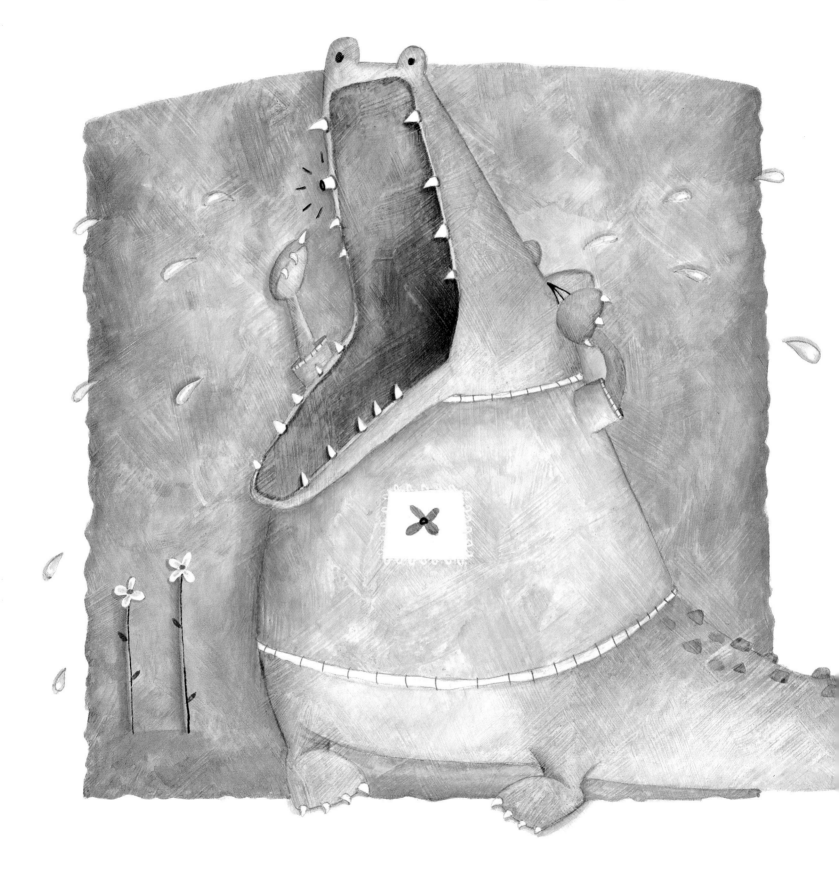

She broke her tooth biting a rhino's bottom.

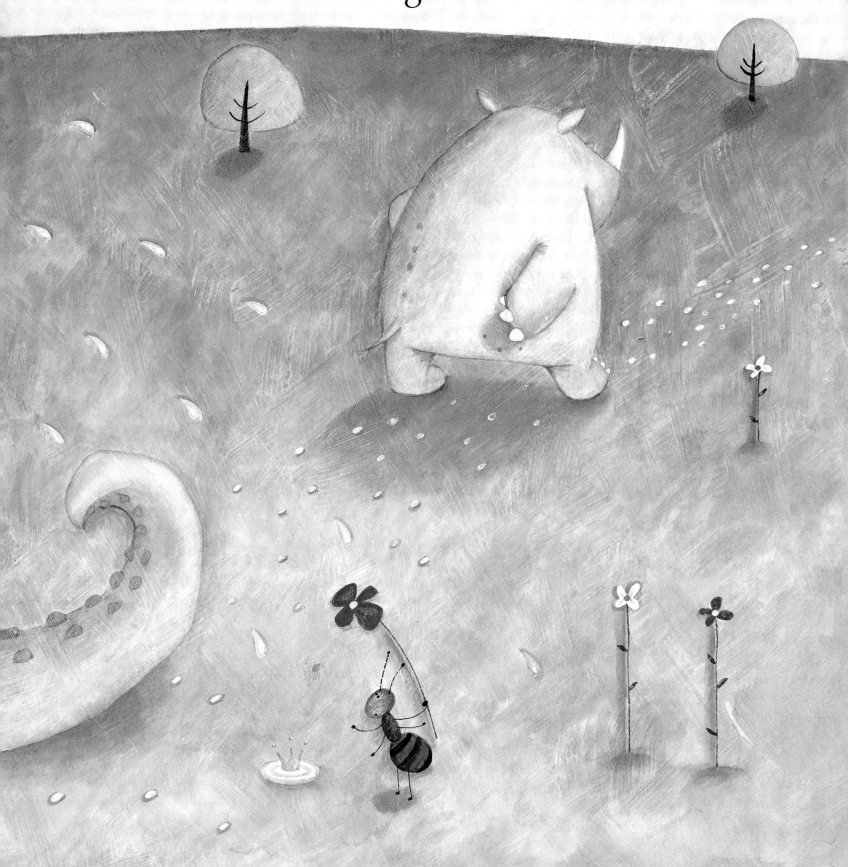

Delia the dragon is poorly.

She sneezed and set fire to her jumper.

BUT THEY ALL TOOK THEIR MEDICINE,
AND THEY ALL GOT BETTER IN...

...THE END.

More Red Fox picture books
for you to enjoy

ELMER
by David McKee 0099697203

MUMMY LAID AN EGG
by Babette Cole 0099299119

RUNAWAY TRAIN
by Benedict Blathwayt 0099385716

DOGGER
by Shirley Hughes 009992790X

WHERE THE WILD THINGS ARE
by Maurice Sendak 0099408392

OLD BEAR
by Jane Hissey 0099265761

MISTER MAGNOLIA
by Quentin Blake 0099400421

ALFIE GETS IN FIRST
by Shirley Hughes 0099855607

OI! GET OFF OUR TRAIN
by John Burningham 009985340X

GORGEOUS
by Caroline Castle and Sam Childs 0099400766

Also by Kes Gray in Red Fox:
Eat Your Peas 0099404672